TEN MONKEY JAMBOREE

by Dianne Ochiltree
pictures by Anne-Sophie Lanquetin

SIMON & SCHUSTER

TO JIM — LIFE WITH YOU IS A JAMBOREE!
— D. O.

POUR MARITÉ ET PIERRE
— ANNE-SOPHIE LANQUETIN

SIMON AND SCHUSTER
First published in Great Britain in 2001 by Simon & Schuster UK Ltd
222 Gray's Inn Road, London WC1X 8HB

Text copyright © 2001 by Diane Ochiltree
Illustrations copyright © 2001 by Anne-Sophie Lanquetin

A CIP catalogue record for this book is available from the British Library upon request

ISBN 978-0-74346-203-7

Printed in Hong Kong

10 9 8 7 6 5 4 3 2

One monkey swings in a jungle tree.

"Monkeys, monkeys.

Play with me!

Monkey fun takes more than one.

Won't you join my jamboree?"

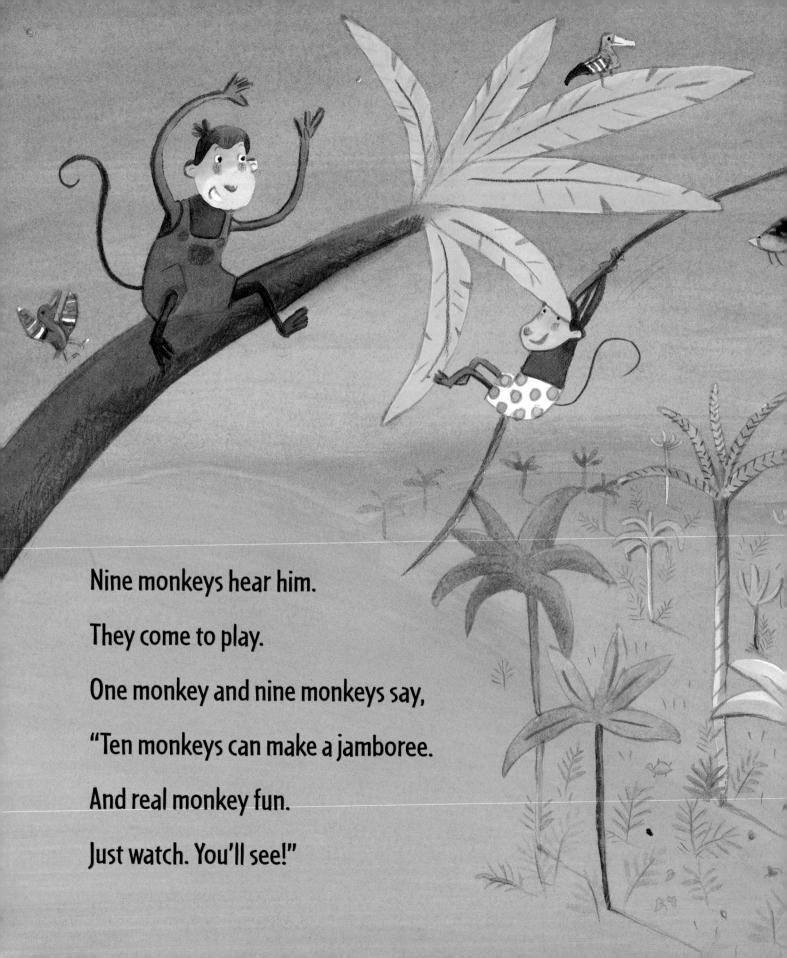

Nine monkeys hear him.

They come to play.

One monkey and nine monkeys say,

"Ten monkeys can make a jamboree.

And real monkey fun.

Just watch. You'll see!"

Seven monkeys leap

from tree to tree.

They twist and spin.

Then leap again.

Two monkeys twirl and flip.

Their long tails curl.

They never slip!

One monkey hangs by her knees

in the breeze.

Ten monkeys have a tail-tangling, tree-dangling jungle jamboree.

Two monkeys click sticks.

The music goes ping ping ping!

Four monkeys swing palm leaves that whistle and sing.

Add four more monkeys to keep the beat.

They slap an old log with hands and feet.

Ten monkeys have a music-making, leaf-shaking jungle jamboree.

Three monkeys dance on a banana-tree branch.

They flip and flop.

They hop.

Then **PLOP**!

A great big bunch falls off for lunch.

Two monkeys munch mountains of berries.

Five monkeys crunch crispy green leaves.

Ten monkeys have a foot-stomping, snack-chomping jungle jamboree.

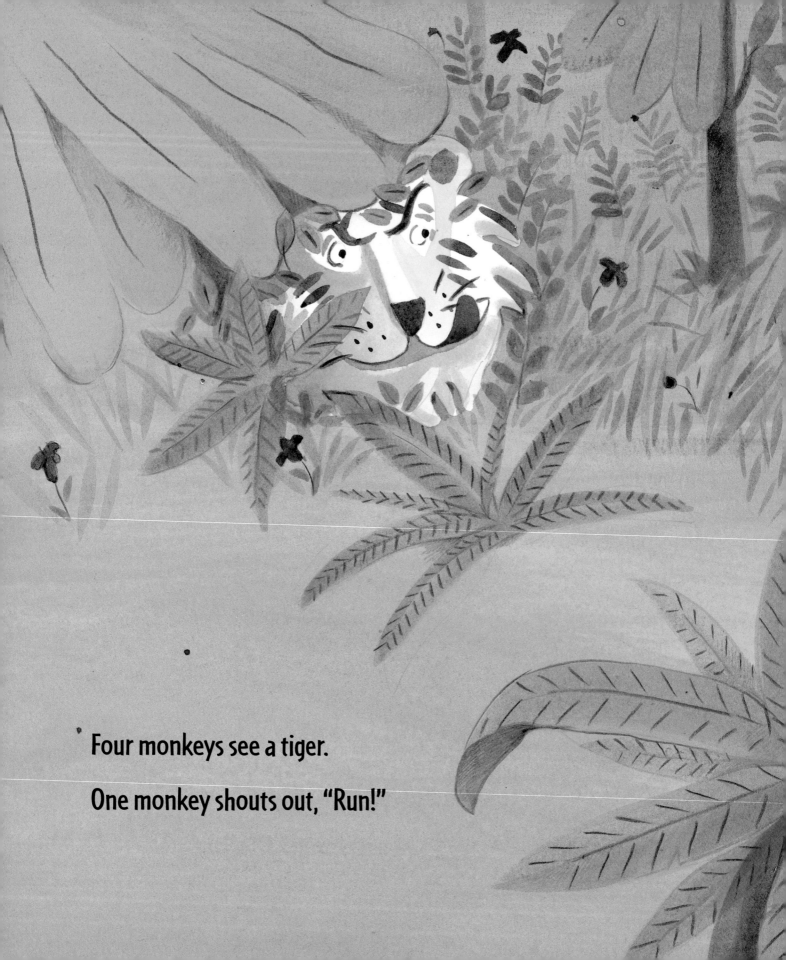

Four monkeys see a tiger.

One monkey shouts out, "Run!"

Five monkeys drop their nuts and stones and stop their monkey fun.

Ten monkeys scramble through the bramble.

They run from paws that snatch and claws that scratch.

Ten monkeys have a

tiger-racing, monkey-chasing jungle jamboree.

One by one, they hug the jungle tree.

Now **WHUMP, WHUMP, WHUMP!**

The monkeys jump up.

They climb up high, far from the trap

of tiger jaws that snarl and snap.

Six monkeys screech and show their teeth.

One monkey spits, chatters and chits.

Three monkeys wave to show they are brave.

Ten monkeys have an **EAR—SPLITTING,** tree-sitting jungle jamboree.

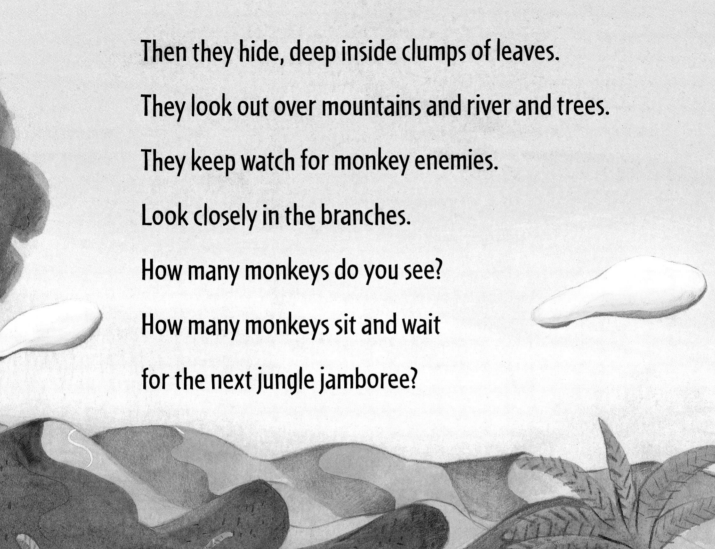

Then they hide, deep inside clumps of leaves.

They look out over mountains and river and trees.

They keep watch for monkey enemies.

Look closely in the branches.

How many monkeys do you see?

How many monkeys sit and wait

for the next jungle jamboree?